KT-872-782

Dancing for Captain Drake

Tudor stories linking with the History
National Curriculum Key Stage 2

For Henry Keane

LEEDS METROPOLITAN
UNIVERSITY LIBRARY
170161 5098
KT-B
823176
JF WAL
17 DEC 1996 free /m/

First published in 1996 by Watts Books
96 Leonard Street, London EC2A 4RH
Watts Books Australia 14 Mars Road, Lane
Cove, NSW 2006

© Karen Wallace 1996
The right of Karen Wallace to be identified as
the Author of this Work has been asserted by
her in accordance with the Copyright, Designs
and Patents Act, 1988

Series editor: Paula Borton
Consultant: Joan Blyth
Designed by Kirstie Billingham
A CIP catalogue record for this book
is available from the British Library.
ISBN 0 7496 2234 2
Dewey Classification 942.05
Printed in Great Britain

Leeds Metropolitan University

Leeds Metropolitan University

17 0164509 8

Dancing for Captain Drake

by
Karen Wallace

Illustrations by Martin Remphry

W
FRANKLIN WATTS
LONDON • NEW YORK • SYDNEY

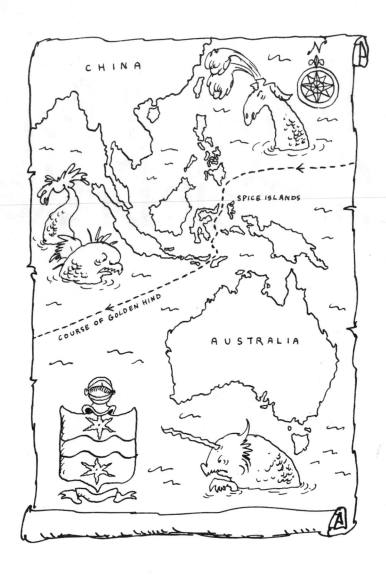

1

What's in a Name?

Arthur Knucklebone sat in the dark sail locker of the *Golden Hind*. In one hand he held a large sailor's needle and in the other hand, the end of a patch. Except that it was more like a bed sheet than a patch. Arthur pushed the needle through

the rough, stinking material. It was bad
enough having to sew on the patch. But it
was worse when you didn't have a clue
how to sew.

Arthur sighed and tried to remember
why he had run off to sea in the first place.
It had all started when his mother had

told him his great-grandfather had done
exactly the same thing with their next door
neighbour, a man called Jack Jones.

Then the most extraordinary
coincidence had happened. Jack Jones's
great-grandson who was also called Jack
Jones had joined the very same ship.

Footsteps clumped down the passage. Arthur looked up. Jack Jones was standing in the doorway. The dusty light from the porthole sparkled on the brass buttons of his cabin boy's blue jacket.

"Bet you'll never guess what I had for supper," he crowed.

Arthur shrugged. If it hadn't been for Jack Jones's dirty tricks, Arthur would have been a cabin boy, not a dogsbody mending sails.

"Captain Drake gave *me* a chicken leg," said Jack

Jones. He dug in his
pocket and threw
Arthur a well-
gnawed bone.
"I left you some."

"I'd rather go hungry
than eat your leftovers," said Arthur,
chucking the bone over his shoulder.

"Huh!" said Jack. "My Mam always
said Knucklebones thought they were
better than Jones." He shoved his weaselly
face into the sail locker. "But I'm better
than you, I am."

Arthur jumped up and dropped his
needle. "You're a cheat and liar is what
you are," he shouted. "Captain Drake
asked *me* to be his cabin boy, not *you*."

Jack Jones smirked. "So what?" he
said. "I bin to school and you ain't."

He turned on his heel. "And that puts me before you, *always.*" Arthur slumped back into his pile of sails. It had all been horribly unfair. Jack Jones had told Cudgel, the first mate, that J for Jones came before K for Knucklebone in the alphabet so *he* should have Arthur's job. And Cudgel was stupid enough to believe him.

"ARTHUR KNUCKLEBONE!"

It was Cudgel's unmistakable bellow.

Thump! Something squashy landed on Arthur's head. It was a pair of white breeches and a blue jacket with two rows of brass buttons.

"Captain's cabin boy's bin sacked," yelled Cudgel.

"You mean Jack Jones?" asked Arthur, hope rising like a bird in his chest.

"Not 'im, the other one," shouted Cudgel. Arthur could hardly believe his luck. "When do I start?" he cried.

"Now! You great booby!" replied Cudgel. "Captain Drake is waiting!"

2

A Firm Handshake is a Fine Thing

"What are *you* doing here?" snarled Jack Jones when Arthur appeared outside Captain Drake's cabin. "Where's Bobby Sixpence?"

"He's gone," replied Arthur. "I'm taking his place."

"You best learn some manners, then," sneered Jack Jones, sticking his chin in the air. "Some of us are born with 'em. Some of us ain't."

"You best watch your mouth," muttered Arthur. "Some of us got teeth. Some of us lose 'em."

Across the water, the islands were edged with palm trees. The sky was the deepest blue he had ever seen and green hills shone in the sun like huge lumps of emerald. Arthur breathed in deeply. The *Golden Hind* had been at anchor for three days. But it was the first time Arthur had stood on deck.

The islands were the Spice Islands and they were famous for their cloves. They were Captain Drake's last trading stop before the long journey back to Plymouth.

Arthur looked down at the main deck. Groups of sailors sat mending ropes while gunners cleaned the heavy guns and

artillery that had to be kept greased and protected from the salt water.

A galley sped across the water towards the ship. Under its canopy a man dressed in long robes lay back on red cushions. "Who's that?" asked Arthur.

"His name is Don Evilio and he's the Portuguese Envoy," replied Jack as if Arthur had asked a really stupid question. "What's a Portuguese Envoy

doing in the Spice Islands?" asked Arthur. "I thought they had a Sultan for their ruler."

"The Spice Islands are a Portuguese colony," sneered Jack Jones. "Don Evilio can do what he wants."

A drum roll sounded.

"Come on," said Jack. "That means we're wanted."

They ran down a ladder into the Great Cabin at the end of the ship. The walls were polished oak and there were windows on all sides. Paintings, some of them by Francis Drake himself, hung on the wooden panelling.

At one end stood a massive oak table laid with silver plates and goblets. Four candlesticks stood like four miniature trees down the middle.

On a raised platform, a small group
of musicians played folk tunes popular in
England at the time they had set sail.

Arthur gasped. He had never seen
such luxury in all his life.

From out of the shadows stepped a
stocky man with a red beard and bright
blue eyes. He laughed when he saw the
expression on Arthur's face. "I'm pleased
you approve of my quarters, young man,"
he said.

Then to Arthur's amazement he stretched out his hand. "Francis Drake," he said, smiling.

"Arthur Knucklebone," replied Arthur. And he took the Captain's hand in his own and shook it firmly.

Francis Drake turned to two gentlemen behind him.

"Here's a lad with a fine handshake," he said. "Good luck to him."

Arthur bowed and backed against the wall. He recognized the two men. One was red-faced with crinkly brown hair and jowls like a bloodhound. His name was Sir Thomas Mutton-Thomas. According to the gossip in the crew's quarters, he was as woolly headed as the sheep he kept on his Devon estate.

The other gentleman was dressed in rose-pink breeches that were too tight and a frilly ruff that was almost as wide as his shoulders. He breathed from a scent bottle he held to his nose and his face was white

with chalk powder.

"Ah, my Lord Poutworthy," cried Francis Drake. "The perfume of our good ship is still not to your liking, I see."

Lord Poutworthy bowed and managed the smallest of smiles so as not to crack his face powder.

On the main deck, a trumpet blew a salute.

Arthur watched as Drake's face changed from jolly captain to cunning host.

"Come gentlemen," he said. "Tho' we would rather trade with the Sultan, himself, we must first seem to listen to this Portuguese Envoy."

"Don't you mess up nothing," hissed Jack Jones as they waited for the Captain to return. "I happens to know this Don Evilio is a very important person. And this is a very important meeting."

Arthur stared at him. "You told me you didn't know anything about him," he said, slowly.

At that moment Don Evilio appeared in the cabin. He had a needle-nosed face and the hard black eyes of a snake. Jack Jones stepped forward and bowed, and to Arthur's amazement, he saw Jack's and Don Evilio's eyes meet. It was almost as if they knew each other.

3

A Plate of Sweet Fish

Francis Drake picked up a silver goblet and filled it with wine. "Welcome to the *Golden Hind*, Don Evilio," he said.

Don Evilio looked round at the richly decorated cabin. His hard eyes took in the table covered in silver and the oak

panelling hung with paintings
of far-off places. He was not
going to be upstaged by this
English pirate who called
himself an Admiral in the
Queen of England's Navy.
He ignored the goblet of
wine and snapped his fingers.

The young boy who had been
on the galley stepped
forward. His eyes were
wide with fear. "Miguel
will see to my
needs, sir,"
he replied,
rudely.

Francis Drake showed Don Evilio to
a chair at the table. "Tell me of the Sultan
of these islands," he said, smiling. "We
would trade with him. Is he a man to be
trusted?"

"He is a savage," replied Don Evilio.
As he spoke he speared a piece of fish with
his knife. "Salt," he demanded, snapping
his fingers.

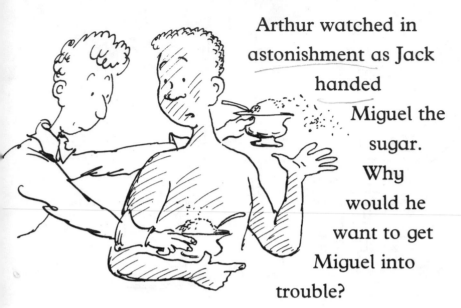

Arthur watched in astonishment as Jack handed Miguel the sugar. Why would he want to get Miguel into trouble?

Just as Miguel was about to sprinkle Don Evilio's fish with sugar, Arthur grabbed the salt and put it into his hands.

Jack's face went dark with anger. Miguel looked between them and understood what had happened. With the slightest nod of his head, he thanked Arthur. Then he gave Jack a look of pure poison.

"I, too, shall have some salt,"
announced Francis Drake, staring at Jack
Jones. "Perhaps Jack's services will be
more fitting when puddings are served."
He held out his goblet for more wine.

Arthur picked up a flagon from the
sideboard. He didn't see Jack stick out his
foot. The next second the flagon tumbled
towards Don Evilio's neck.

In the same second, Miguel grabbed hold of it and served Francis Drake himself.

Drake smiled as if he had noticed nothing. "You were speaking of the Sultan, Don Evilio," he murmured.

"A tyrant and a cheat," cried Don Evilio. "Not fit to trade with a gentleman, like yourself." The hard black eyes glittered in his face. "But I have a rich store of cloves and other spices in my palace. I would be honoured if you would join me for a banquet tomorrow."

Francis Drake raised his eyebrows and pretended to swallow the contents of his goblet. "A banquet and a great quantity of cloves?" he cried. "This is good news indeed."

Don Evilio raised his own goblet. "A toast to a fine trade between our two

countries," he said smoothly.

"To a fine trade," replied Francis
Drake raising his goblet. "Come!" he cried
to the musicians. "This is a celebration!
Play us your merriest tune!"

Later, that night Arthur pulled off the
blue jacket and hung it on a spike. He
would have preferred to hang Jack Jones.
In fact every time he thought of Jack
Jones, his fists clenched in anger. It was

almost as if Jack Jones had wanted to ruin the evening to impress Don Evilio.

But why?

❖

Arthur crawled into a small space between two sails and closed his eyes. Captain Drake's last words echoed in his mind. *You're a good lad, Arthur,* he had said. *If you ever have any troubles, come to me, first.*

4

True or False

TAP! TAP! TAP!

Arthur sat bolt upright, his heart
hammering in his chest. A man's face
loomed out of the porthole. Two white eyes
glowed in the moonlight and something
like a bone was clenched in his teeth.

Arthur watched, frozen with horror, as two hands appeared and the man pulled himself through the porthole and landed lightly on the floor.

"Who are you?" cried Arthur in a hoarse whisper.

"I have a message from the Sultan," said the man in a low urgent voice. He handed Arthur a roll of parchment. "You must give it to your Captain. His life depends on it."

Footsteps creaked in the passageway.

The man quickly squeezed back through the porthole. "Hurry," he whispered. "There's no time to lose."

A second later, there was a small splash from far below.

A figure holding a lantern appeared in the doorway.

Arthur groaned as if he had just woken up. He rolled in his blanket and stuffed the parchment down the front of his shirt.

 The lantern
crossed the
floor and Jack
Jones stood
over him.

"Who were
you talking to?"
he snarled.

"None of your business, you rat,"
whispered Arthur. He jumped up and with
his right hand, thumped Jack Jones on the
side of the head.

Jack fell to his knees but before Arthur
could hit him again, he grabbed a piece of
rope and whacked Arthur across the
shoulders. Then he stumbled out the
doorway and ran back down the corridor.

Arthur was just about to go after him
when he saw a leather pouch on the floor.

It must have fallen out of Jack's pocket
when he fell.

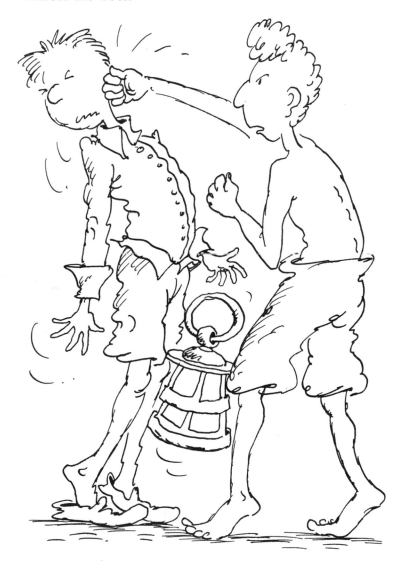

Arthur bent down and opened it up.

Inside were two Portuguese ducats and a small silver dagger. A large E was engraved on the hilt. Arthur stood in the darkness, the dagger in his hand, and the roll of parchment pressed against his chest. Should he tell the Captain? Or was he being used to spring some horrible trap?

He thought of Drake's words. *If you have any troubles. Come to me, first.*

Arthur pulled on the blue jacket and
raced down the corridor.

Light showed under Drake's door.
Arthur took a deep breath and knocked.

"Enter," said a low voice.

Francis Drake was sitting at his desk.
Charts and instruments were spread all
over the top. On the floor his huge leather
bound sea chest was open, bulging with
important-looking documents.

Francis Drake looked up. His face was lined with worry and the blue eyes were dull with exhaustion. "What is it, lad?" he said.

Arthur's mouth went dry. He stepped forward and held out the parchment in a trembling hand.

"How did you come by this?" asked Drake when he had finished reading.

Arthur told him everything from the moment he had first seen Don Evilio's galley. Finally he showed him the pouch with the silver dagger and the Portuguese ducats.

"It is as I thought," said Francis Drake. He fixed Arthur with his blue eyes. "Tomorrow you and Master Jones will accompany Sir Thomas Mutton-Thomas and my Lord Poutworthy to Don Evilio's palace."

Arthur nodded.

"I shall have a mysterious illness," said Drake in a low voice. "And you, Arthur Knucklebone will be my ears and my eyes. And in doing so, you will represent the Queen of England, herself."

"Yessir," croaked Arthur. Then he fainted and hit his head on the floor.

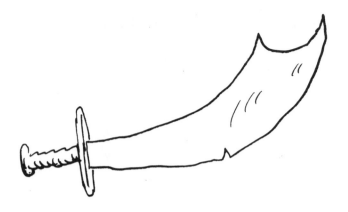

5

Bad Manners Saves the Day

Arthur stood in the banqueting hall of
Don Evilio's palace and gingerly felt the
lump on his head. It had all been rather
embarrassing. Captain Drake himself had
carried him to his bed in the sail locker.
Then the next morning as Arthur had

stepped into the longboat, Drake had whispered. "It's up to you, boy. Do what is necessary."

LEEDS METROPOLITAN UNIVERSITY LIBRARY

There was a sharp pain in his shin.

"Wake up, dullard," hissed Jack Jones. "Sir Thomas wants more wine."

Arthur nodded. He had to pretend he didn't know Jack Jones was a traitor who had promised to spy on his Captain for a bag of gold ducats from the Portuguese Envoy.

Don Evilio sat at the head of a huge table stacked with food. On either side of him, Sir Thomas Mutton-Thomas and Lord Poutworthy stuffed their faces and gulped goblets of wine.

"A sudden sickness, you say," growled Don Evilio.

"Terrible quick, it was," agreed Sir Thomas Mutton-Thomas, cramming six tiny birds stuffed with apricots into his mouth. "Something in the water, no doubt."

"No doubt," said Don Evilio sipping at a

glass of freshly squeezed lemon juice.
He looked as sour and yellow as a lemon
himself.

"Your palace is quite splendid, Don
Evilio," cried Lord Poutworthy. "And I
must congratulate you on the
sweetness of your island's air."

"Must you," snarled Don Evilio.

"And when do the doctors say your Captain will recover?"

"On the morrow, dear sir," spluttered Sir Thomas, spraying the table with bits of bone and apricot.

"Even sooner, perhaps," added Lord Poutworthy, hiding two mangoes in his breeches' pocket.

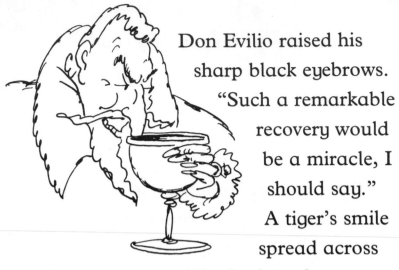 Don Evilio raised his
sharp black eyebrows.
"Such a remarkable
recovery would
be a miracle, I
should say."
A tiger's smile
spread across
his face. It was as if he had made some
important decision.

"Come, come," he cried. "*Everyone*
must enjoy the riches of my table. Miguel,
fill two plates for the Captain's loyal
servants."

"J before K," hissed Jack and he
grabbed the first plate and stuffed his
mouth with food.

Miguel filled a second plate. As he
handed it to Arthur, he stared at him and

with the quickest of movements, he pulled
down one eyelid and rolled his eyes.

Suddenly Arthur understood why
Don Evilio was only drinking lemon juice.

The food was drugged or even worse,
it was poisoned.

Arthur took the plate with trembling
hands. What on earth was he going to
do, now?

How could he not eat without making

Don Evilio suspicious?

Then he remembered mealtimes in his mother's house. *Sit up straight. Get your hair out of your plate. I can't even see what you're eating!*

Arthur slouched over the table, propped his head up with one hand and let his hair fall into his plate.

Now nobody could see that he wasn't eating!

There was only one problem.

Everyone else had fallen face first into their plates.

"Your game is up, you cunning English pup," snarled Don Evilio. He strode towards him. A long curved sword glittered in his hand.

Luckily for Arthur, Don Evilio didn't

see Miguel's foot stretched out in front of
him. He swung his sword high in the air,
then with a bellow of rage, he tripped and
fell over.

Quick as a flash, Miguel dropped a
huge flagon of wine on his head. And just
like the others, Don Evilio's eyes rolled
back and he lay still.

"Follow me," cried Miguel. "The
Sultan is waiting!"

Arthur raced
down a tiled
hall and
followed
Miguel into
some
sort of
dressing
chamber.

"If you want to trade cloves you have to put these on," he said handing Arthur a pair of baggy gold trousers and a shiny silver top.

"But these are for *dancing-girls*," cried Arthur in disgust.

"The Sultan *likes* dancing," hissed Miguel "No dancing. No deal."

Captain Drake's words sounded in Arthur's mind. *Do what is necessary.* Arthur climbed into the clothes and tied a see-through veil around his head. He had never felt so *silly* in all of his life.

6

Dancing for Captain Drake

"Greetings, Oh, Great One," cried
Arthur. And exactly as Miguel had
instructed him, he threw himself on the
floor.

The Sultan grinned from ear to ear.
He was huge and wore baggy silk trousers

and turquoise slippers with gold bobbles on the end.

"May the sun forever shine on your venerable vastness," mumbled Arthur from the floor. He crawled forward and kissed the gold bobbles.

"Arise, Englishman of exquisite manners and excellent dress sense," cried the Sultan. "Arise and dance in the English fashion."

The Sultan's eyes went hard. "For I would see it *before* you leave my island."

Then to Arthur's total astonishment,

Miguel tied a string of bells
around each of his knees.

"What's he talking
about?" whispered
Arthur, desperately.

Miguel rolled
his eyes and
handed him
three silk
handkerchiefs.

"Morris Dancing, you idiot," he hissed.

Arthur stared open-mouthed. *"Morris
Dancing!* Of course!"

But how did Miguel know?

In fact, how did Miguel seem to know
everything?

But there was no time for questions.
Arthur jumped up and down kicked his feet.
He waved the handkerchief and spun in circles.

The Sultan was delighted. He clapped his hands. Miguel tied two identical strings of bells round his vast knees and pressed an extra large handkerchief into his hand.

Arthur leapt up again. He did two terrible cartwheels. He knocked his knees together and in a fit of excitement stuffed a handkerchief in his mouth.

The Sultan jumped down from his throne. He pounded across the room, throwing his legs in the air and waved his handkerchief about as if it was on fire.

Dust floated down from the ceiling as the vast pillars that held up the roof began to wobble.

The Sultan danced and danced but he said nothing about trading cloves.

Time was running out. Arthur slapped his heels together, twirled in a circle and jumped on his handkerchief. "Captain Drake wants six tons of cloves by tomorrow's tide!" he shouted.

The Sultan spun like a top, slipped on his handkerchief, crashed onto the floor and slid the entire length of the room.

All the servants stared in horror. Even Miguel was holding his breath. The only sound was the steady pattering of plaster from the ceiling.

The Sultan's face was the colour of beetroot and tears of delight were pouring down his vast wobbly cheeks. "Captain Drake shall have his cloves by tomorrow's tide!" cried the Sultan. "Your dance has

pleased me greatly."

"Hurry!" cried Miguel, grabbing Arthur by his trousers.

"The tide is turning! Your galley is waiting!" They raced back through the palace and down to the harbour.

Sure enough, a galley bobbed on the water, its oars raised, ready to leave.

Arthur jumped on board.

To his surprise, Miguel stayed on the shore.

"Aren't you coming, too?" he shouted.

Miguel shook his head and grinned.

Suddenly all the questions in Arthur's mind tumbled out of his mouth. "What about Don Evilio?" he shouted.

"Don Evilio is a traitor and now we have proof," replied Miguel.

"We?" gasped Arthur.

"I work for the Sultan," replied Miguel. "And I am also a great admirer of your English country dances."

"Sir Thomas Mutton-Thomas and Lord Poutworthy!" cried Arthur. "I can't leave them behind!"

A strange choking noise came from a large woven basket behind him. "We're here," mumbled Sir Thomas Mutton-Thomas.

"And we don't feel very well," moaned Lord Poutworthy.

There was one more question in Arthur's mind.

"What will happen to Jack Jones?" he yelled.

There was a wicked gleam in Miguel's eyes. "He'll have to learn Portuguese!" he said with a shout of laughter. Then Miguel disappeared into the palm trees.

Arthur turned. The *Golden Hind* floated like a castle in front of him. On the top deck, outside the Captain's Cabin, stood the stocky figure of Francis Drake.

Their eyes met and the Captain raised the goblet in his hand. A roar of congratulations bounced like a cannon ball over the water.

Francis Drake

Early days

Francis Drake was born
in 1541 in Devon. He
had bright blue eyes
and red hair. He was one of 12 sons.

His first job was on a merchant ship trading
across the Channel. His first expedition to the
Spanish colonies in South and Central America
was in 1567. There he saw the Pacific Ocean
for the first time. He returned with a cargo of
stolen gold and jewels.

The great expedition

Arthur Knucklebone's story
is make-believe, but
Drake's expedition on the
Golden Hind was very
real. Francis Drake
started out in 1577.

His orders were to travel around the world and steal as much gold as he could.

The expedition took almost three years! On his way back, Drake stopped at the Spice Islands in Indonesia. The islands were a Portuguese colony and because of this only Portugal could sell the valuable cloves they produced. But Drake made a deal with the Sultan of the Spice Islands and bought six tonnes worth!

Overboard

On the last leg of the journey, the *Golden Hind* struck a reef and became trapped. She was heavy in the water because of all the gold and jewels Drake had stolen! To free the boat, Drake threw overboard most of the cloves and some heavy guns.

A great man

Sir Francis Drake made many more expeditions.
He also helped destroy the Spanish Armada that
tried to invade England in 1588.

Sir Francis Drake died
in 1596. He was buried at
sea. His drum and sea
chest that he took with him
on all his voyages can still
be seen at Buckland
Abbey, in Devon.

Cloves

In Tudor times, cloves were worth their weight in
gold. The Elizabethans did not have refrigerators
so they used spices, such as cloves, to preserve
their food. Elizabethans also had very bad
teeth and cloves are a good
medicine for toothache.